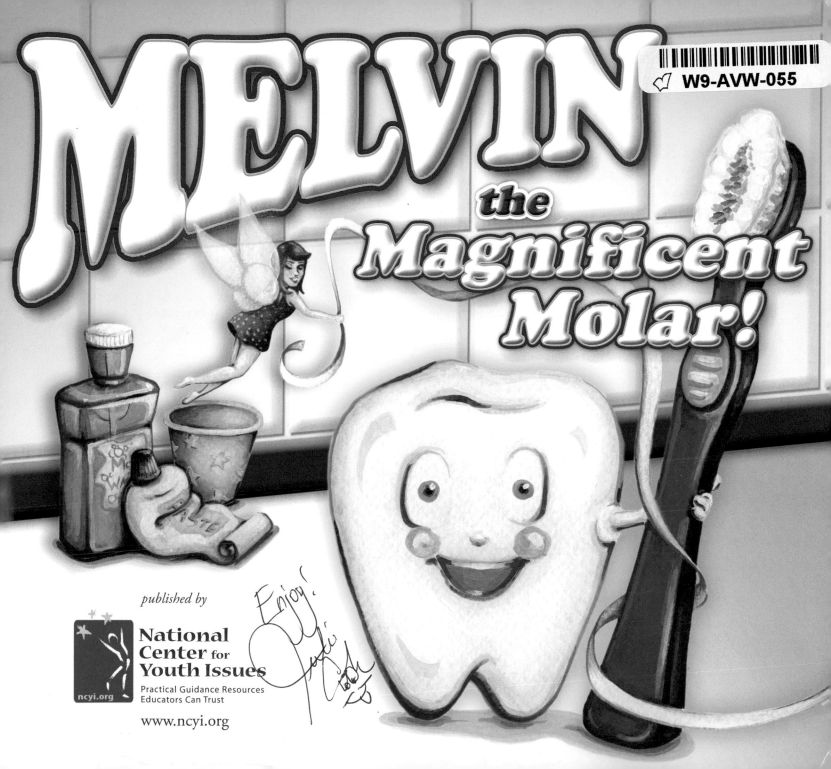

A special thanks to Victoria Markel!

–Julia and Laura

Duplication and Copyright

P.O. Box 22185
Chattanooga, TN 37422-2185
423.899.5714 • 800.477.8277
fax: 423.899.4547
www.ncyi.org

ISBN: 978-1-931636-74-2
© 2010 National Center for Youth Issues, Chattanooga, TN
All rights reserved.

Written by: Julia Cook and Laura Jana, MD.
Illustrations by: Allison Valentine
Page Layout by: Phillip W. Rodgers
Published by National Center for Youth Issues
Softcover

Printed at RR Donnelley • Reynosa, Tamaulipas, Mexico • March 2010

About This Book

Taking good care of your teeth is one of the best things you can do to stay healthy. Unfortunately, teaching children this important message can be quite a challenge. Since teeth that are uncared for can cause pain, missed school, and even serious illness, we have created this book to help all children enjoy learning about taking care of their teeth.

Meet Melvin...the lovable tooth.

Melvin will speak to your child from a tooth's point of view, explaining all that is involved with maintaining a healthy smile. He shows children the importance of visiting the dentist every 6 months beginning at the age of one; that taking good care of their baby (primary) teeth matters; when to use fluoride toothpaste and how much to use (no more than a tiny dab the size of a toddler's pinky fingernail); and what to expect during a trip to see the dentist and dental hygienist.

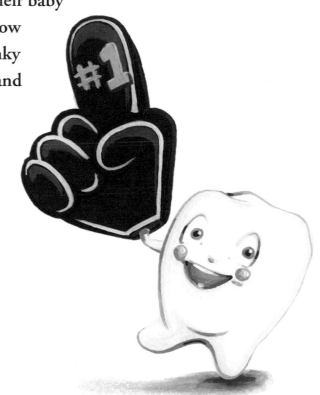

It is our belief that in order to teach a child, you must enter their view of the world. Melvin the Magnificent Molar is a unique children's book that can do just that! We have had a great time creating this book and hope that it will make a positive difference in the lives and the smiles of all who read it!

All the best -

Julia Cook & Dr. Laura Jana

P.S. Brush your Melvin!

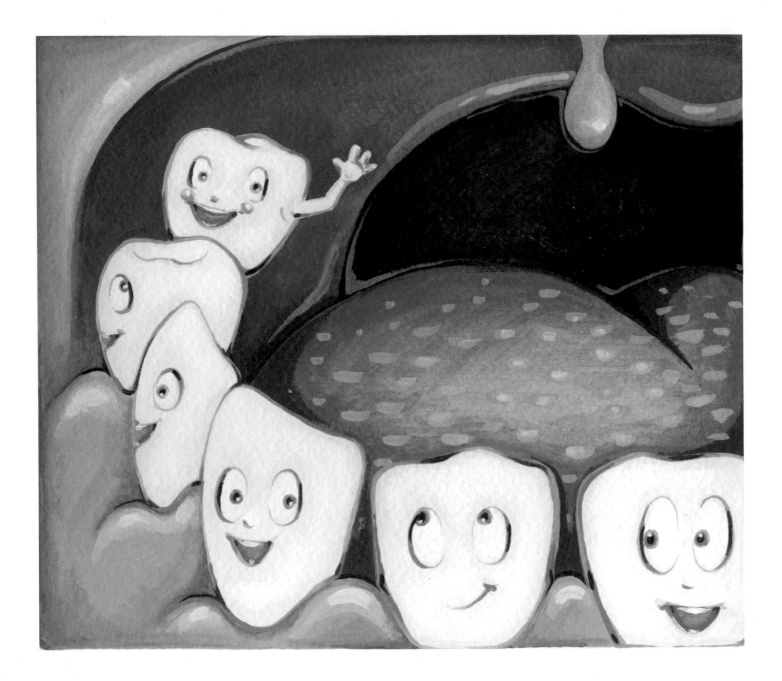

My name is Melvin the Magnificent Molar!

I am a tooth and I live way, **way**, way
in the back of your mouth.
I'm pretty new around here,
But I already have lots of friends.

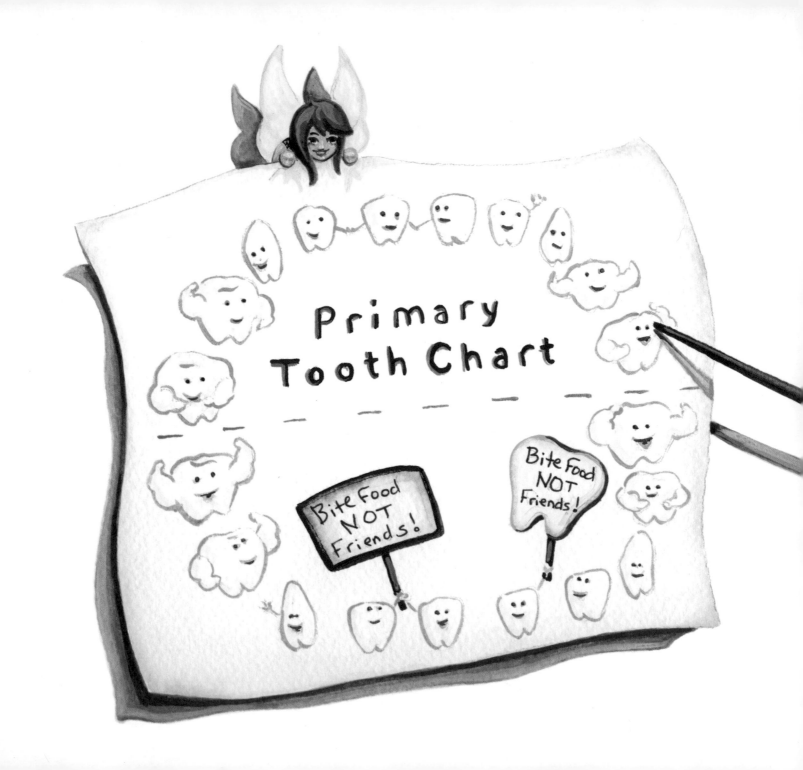

A couple of my friends are big chewers, just like me.
Then there are my little friends up front.
They like to just hang out all day and smile.
Well, that's not all they do.

Their other job is to bite…

food that is,
not people!

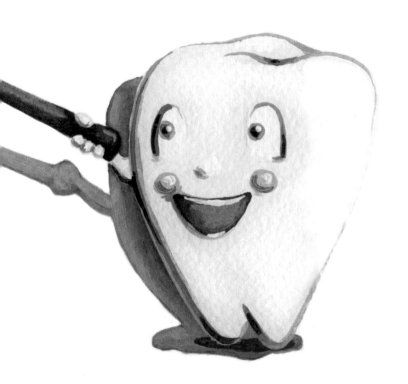

Sometimes I get called a "baby tooth."
That makes me SO mad!

I am a primary tooth.

As in **primary**...

NUMERO UNO!!

That's me,

**Mister
A#1!**

I am **magnificent** and I'm also **very important!**

It's my job to get things ready around here and hold a place
for the permanent tooth that will live here after I leave.

You get to practice taking care of me so that when
your permanent tooth does move in, you'll know
just how to treat him.

Floss

1) Brush
2) Floss
3) Swish
4) Spit
5) Visit Dentist every 6 months

If you do a good job, you'll get to keep him for a lifetime.

Most of the time, I am very happy. The first thing I do every morning when I wake up is sing the "Happy Tooth" song with all of my friends. It goes like this:

I am a tooth and I'm part of a team

We chew and we smile

And we love to be clean!

There's front teeth and back teeth, some big and some small
We all are important! So help us stand tall!

Brush us and floss us and help us to shine,

so we can be ready and look mighty fine

when we finally get to meet...

The Tooth Fairy!

Usually before we get all the way thru our Happy Tooth song,
The Amazing Toothbrush shows up and gives us our morning bath.

With a dab of toothpaste
and a soft bristle-brush scrub,
It feels so good to get
the sleeping scummies off!

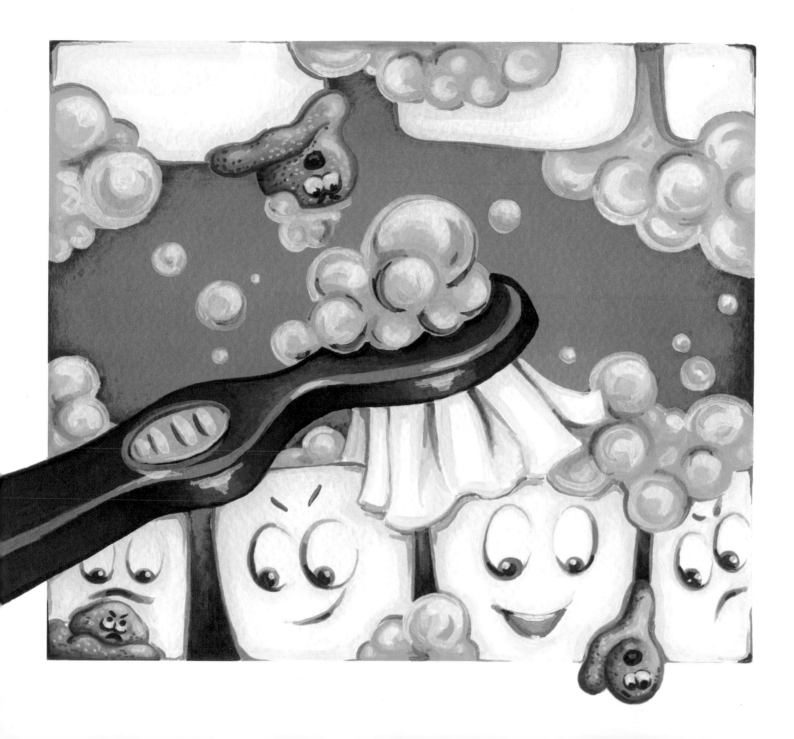

The smiling teeth up front always get a great bath
But since I'm stuck clear in the back, I sometimes get missed.
It really bugs me when that happens
So I start to yell…

"Help me! Help me! I need to get clean!"

The sleeping scummies are turning me **GREEN**
Please brush me, please floss me, please swish them away.
Don't let the scummies bug me all day!

That usually works.

Ever since I erupted on the scene a couple of months ago,
I've heard the smiling teeth up front talk about going
to the dentist. They've already been a whole bunch of
times and they say that it's the coolest thing ever!

They tell me that dentists care about every tooth,
The ones that are tight and the ones that are loose.
They check to make sure that we're being kept clean.
The last thing they want is for us to turn green.

And guess what else?

I've heard that our dentist is even friends with...

The
Tooth
Fairy!

Today, I finally got to go and see for myself.

The smiling teeth were right…
I felt just like a movie star, spotlight and all!
The light was so bright I had to put on my shades!

They even took
my picture!

We all wanted to show the dentist our very best sparkle and shine,
so we all signed up for a VIT (Very Important Tooth) Treatment.

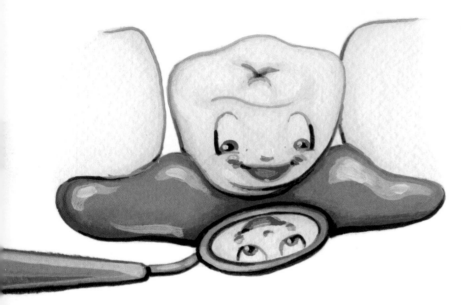

A **mirror** came in first
that was hooked to a stick.

It looked all around
and was in and out quick.

A **squirt gun** came in and
got us all wet,

But that didn't last long, so we
didn't fret.

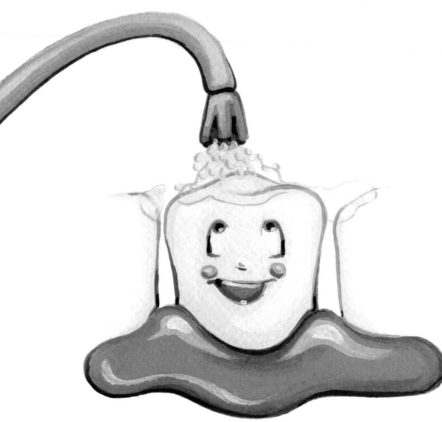

Mister Thirsty came in
and sucked everything dry.

I didn't get scared,
and I didn't cry.

Next came the **Scaler.**

It's like a broom that
sweeps plaque.

I didn't mind it at all.
I love a good scratch.

Mr. Thirsty and the squirt gun came in once again.

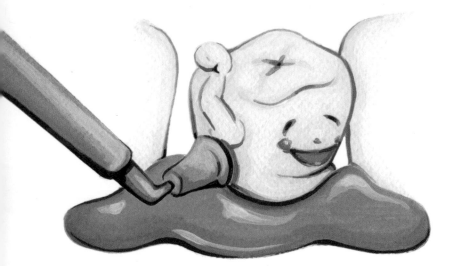

Then **Miss Tickles**,
the polisher, shined me
and my friends.

After Miss Tickles had given us gloss,

The **Magic String** came in
and gave us a floss.

And to top it all off,

We got a brand new **coat of fluoride** to make us all stronger.

With star treatment like that we're sure to last longer!

And then…

the *big*
moment
happened...

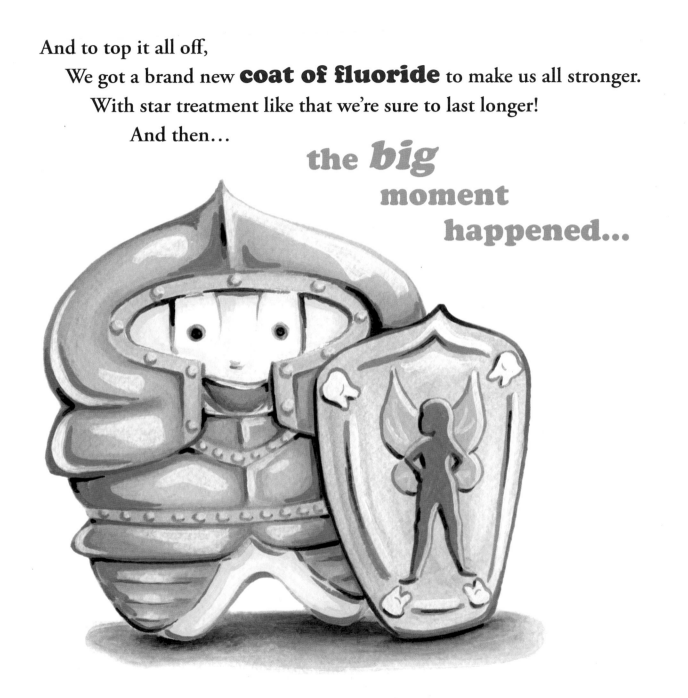

In came the DENTIST!

He wore a royal white robe and
had a jeweled crown on his head.

We showed him our very, very, very best
behavior, and he just loved it!

He used his regal pointer to
count each and every one of us —
his loyal subjects.

And then he gave us all
an official DDS inspection!

We were all MAGNIFICENT!

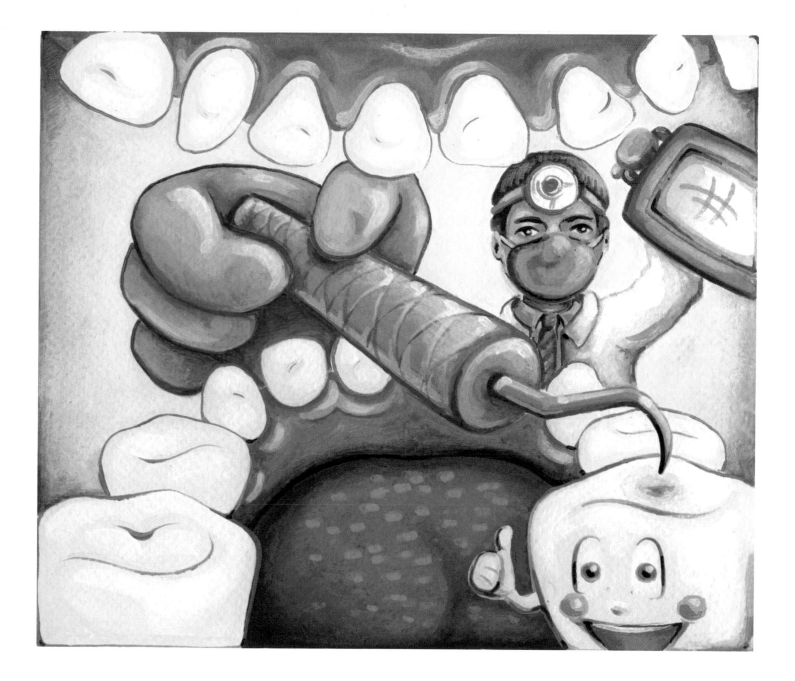

As a reward, we got the one thing that all teeth dream about:

An amazing new toothbrush!

It's a good thing, too, because our old one
isn't so amazing anymore.

The other day I noticed it seemed
a little bent out of shape,
and I'm pretty sure I saw
a few sleeping scummies stuck to it.

DDS
Inspection
~Graduate~
Next Appointment
in 6 months...
X December 14

I am **Melvin** the **Magnificent Molar**
and I am **SO proud** to be your tooth!

Thank you so much
for keeping me clean.

With all of your help,
I will never turn grccn.

I'm a happy tooth now
and because of you
I know that my tooth-dreams
will surely come true…

Hey Grown-ups!

You can have **America's Toothfairy®** send a personalized, autographed letter to a special child in your life thanking them for taking good care of their teeth!

Visit www.AmericasToothfairy.org and make a positive difference for a child in need today! With your $10 tax-deductible donation, America's Toothfairy® will send your child a personalized letter and you will become an official Toothfairy helper by making it possible for another child to receive critical dental care.

About America's Toothfairy® Campaign

The *America's Toothfairy®* Campaign is a dedicated effort of National Children's Oral Health Foundation, whose mission is to eliminate pediatric dental disease and promote overall health and well being for millions of children from vulnerable populations. Five times more prevalent than asthma, pediatric dental disease and decay is the most common chronic childhood illness in America. Millions of children every day have trouble eating, sleeping and learning because they are in severe pain from easily preventable dental complications.

America's beloved Toothfairy has now assumed a leading role as Educator, Preventer, and Protector –ensuring critical oral health services are available to the children who need them most. 100% of donations to America's Toothfairy® Campaign go to programs that change children's lives. By working through a large network of non-profit Affiliate facilities across the country, over 1 million underserved children have already received critical oral health care and the tools needed for a lifetime of good oral hygiene. With your support, we can work together to give all children a happy, healthy smile – an invaluable gift that will last them a lifetime!

Please visit www.AmericasToothfairy.org and contribute today!

Melvin's Top 10 Tips for Happy, Healthy Teeth

1. Treat baby teeth with the respect they deserve– they are very important!

2. Clean baby's gums with a damp washcloth or baby toothbrush after each feeding even before the first teeth show up.

3. Milk, formula, juice and other sweet drinks can all cause serious tooth decay so never put children to bed with a bottle containing anything but water.

4. Just like grown-up teeth, baby teeth need to be cleaned regularly. Use a soft-bristled baby- or child-friendly toothbrush at least twice each day.

5. Fluoride toothpaste is important for healthy teeth. Just remember it's *tooth* paste, not tummy paste! Teach your child to spit out toothpaste instead of swallowing it and wait to start using toothpaste with fluoride in it until your child is 2 (unless your dentist recommends it sooner). Even then, only use a tiny dab no bigger than your toddler's pinky fingernail until you can be sure your child will spit it out after brushing!

6. Celebrate your child's first birthday with a tooth check-up by a doctor, dentist, or other oral health professional. Beginning at the age of 1, it is recommended that all kids get their teeth checked every 6 months.

7. Start teaching children how to brush and floss early (at the age of two or three), but don't expect them to be able to get their teeth clean all on their own until at least the age of 6 or 7 (or older!).

8. Children need to floss as soon as they have two teeth that touch. Flossing may not be necessary in the first few years, since baby (or *primary*) teeth often have space between them. Be on the lookout, though, since it's often the molars "way, way, way in the back of the mouth" (like Melvin) that touch first.

9. Limit sugary foods and drinks to mealtimes. Offer water and milk between meals, and teach your child to use his tongue to clean food and sleeping scummies off of his teeth between brushing.

10. Remember to make brushing teeth, flossing, and visits to the dentist a fun family affair!